Crime Against Nature is the Lamont Poetry Selection of the Academy of American Poets.

From 1954 through 1974 the Lamont Poetry Selection supported the publication and distribution of twenty first books of poems. Since 1975 this distinguished award has been given for an American poet's second book.

Judges for 1989: *Marvin Bell, Alfred Corn, Sandra McPherson*

Other books by Minnie Bruce Pratt

We Say We Love Each Other

Yours In Struggle: Three Feminist Perspectives on Anti-Semitism and Racism (co-author)

The Sound Of One Fork (chapbook)

CRIME
AGAINST
NATURE

CRIME
AGAINST
NATURE

MINNIE BRUCE PRATT

The Lamont Poetry Selection for 1989

Firebrand
Books
Ithaca, New York

811
P

Slightly different versions of several of these poems have appeared in the following publications: *The American Voice, Gay Community News, Heresies, Out/Look, Ploughshares,* and *Sinister Wisdom.*

This book may not be reproduced in whole or in part, except in the case of reviews, without permission from Firebrand Books, 141 The Commons, Ithaca, New York 14850. ▮▮▮▮▮▮▮▮▮▮▮▮▮▮

Book and cover design by Betsy Bayley
Typesetting by Bets Ltd.

Printed on acid-free paper in the United States by McNaughton & Gunn

Library of Congress Cataloging-in-Publication Data

Pratt, Minnie Bruce.
    Crime against nature.

    I. Title.
PS3566.R35C75   1990   811'.54   90-2778
ISBN 0-932379-73-7
ISBN 0-932379-72-9 (pbk.)

For Ransom and for Ben

Acknowledgments

I thank very much, for their support and editorial comments, Joan E. Biren, Elly Bulkin, Rachel Guido deVries, Laura Flegel, Nanette Gartrell, Rose Gladney, Raymina Y. Mays, Elizabeth Knowlton, Judith McDaniel, Dee Mosbacher, Marcia Winter.

I thank the Community Writer's Project of Syracuse, New York, for the residency which made much of the writing of this book possible.

A grateful thank you to Nancy K. Bereano for her commitment to publishing poetry, her confidence in these poems, and her skillful editing.

Contents

∽

Poem for My Sons

When you were born, all the poets I knew
were men, dads eloquent on their sleeping
babes and the future: Coleridge at midnight,
Yeats' prayer that his daughter lack opinions,
his son be high and mighty, think and act.
You've read the new father's loud eloquence,
fiery sparks written in a silent house
breathing with the mother's exhausted sleep.

When you were born, my first, what I thought was
milk: my breasts sore, engorged, but not enough
when you woke.   With you, my youngest, I did not
think: my head unraised for three days, mind-dead
from waist-down anesthetic labor, saddle
block, no walking either.
                                        Your father was then
the poet I'd ceased to be when I got married.
It's taken me years to write this to you.

I had to make a future, willful, voluble,
lascivious, a thinker, a long walker,
unstruck transgressor, furious, shouting,
voluptuous, a lover, a smeller of blood,
milk, a woman mean as she can be some nights,
existence I could pray to, capable of
poetry.
                Now here we are.   You are men,
and I am not the woman who rocked you
in the sweet reek of penicillin, sour milk,
the girl who could not imagine herself
or a future more than a warm walled room,
had no words but the pap of the expected,
and so, those nights, could not wish for you.

But now I have spoken, my self, I can ask
for you: that you'll know evil when you smell it;
that you'll know good and do it, and see how both
run loose through your lives; that then you'll remember
you come from dirt and history; that you'll choose
memory, not anesthesia; that you'll have work
you love, hindering no one, a path crossing
at boundary markers where you question power;
that your loves will match you thought for thought
in the long heat of blood and fact of bone.

Words not so romantic nor so grandly tossed
as if I'd summoned the universe to be
at your disposal.
                    I can only pray:

That you'll never ask for the weather, earth,
angels, women, or other lives to obey you;

that you'll remember me, who crossed, recrossed
you,
          as a woman making slowly toward
an unknown place where you could be with me,
like a woman on foot, in a long stepping out.

Justice, Come Down

A huge sound waits, bound in the ice,
in the icicle roots, in the buds of snow
on fir branches, in the falling silence
of snow, glittering in the sun, brilliant
as a swarm of gnats, nothing but hovering
wings at midday.   With the sun comes noise.
Tongues of ice break free, fall, shatter,
splinter, speak.   If I could write the words.

Simple, like turning a page, to say *Write*
what happened, but this means a return
to the cold place where I am being punished.
Alone to the stony circle where I am frozen,
the empty space, children, mother, father gone,
lover gone away.   There grief still sits
and waits, grim, numb, keeping company with
anger.   I can smell my anger like sulfur-
struck matches.   I wanted what had happened
to be a wall to burn, a window to smash.
At my fist the pieces would sparkle and fall.
All would be changed.   I would not be alone.

Instead I have told my story over and over
at parties, on the edge of meetings, my life
clenched in my fist, my eyes brittle as glass.

Ashamed, people turned their faces away
from the woman ranting, asking: *Justice,*
stretch out your hand.   Come down, glittering,
from where you have hidden yourself away.

No Place

One night before I left I sat halfway down,
halfway up the stairs, as he reeled at the bottom,
shouting *Choose, choose.*   Man or woman, her or him,
me or the children.   There was no place to be
simultaneous, or between.   Above, the boys slept
with nightlights as tiny consolations in the dark,
like the flowers of starry campion, edge of the water.

The month before I left I dreamed we three waded
across a creek, muddy green, blood warm, quick cold.

I warn the boys of danger, sharp drop-offs, currents,
ledges like knives as we search the water with our feet.
Like the creek at home, late summer, but the opposite
stone wall is gone.   We get across, footing sand
on the other side.   There is milkweed, purple-bronze
wild hydrangea, and an unfamiliar huge openness.
It is the place, promised, that has not yet been,
the place where everything is changed, the place
after the revolution, the revelation, the judgment.
Groups of women pass by, talking, as if we are not
there.   Who can I ask for help?   I am awkward,
at a loss.   We are together, we have come across.
We have no place to go.

                              We had no place to go.
I remember one visit, us traveling crammed
in my Volkswagen, no more room than a closet:
suitcases, model airplanes, an ice chest with food,
my typewriter, books, a bushy fern in a pot,
a spilled pack of cards, pillows and coats spread
in makeshift beds, the children asleep, as I drove
past midnight trying to get to Mama's house
since he would not let them come sleep in mine.

How tired we got of traveling the night land;
how we crossed river after river in the dark,
the Reedy, the Oconee, the Cahaba, all unseen;
how night and the rivers flowed into a huge void
as if that was where we were going, no place at all.

Declared Not Fit

In this month of grief I am crying for my lover.
Suddenly my children appear under my closed eyelids
inside my grief, as if in a pitch-dark room,
vision: apparitions heavy with distance, absence.

I think: This is how you see your past just
before you die.

                    My eyes were the rearview mirror
years ago.   The boys were small and round, waving
good-bye.   Their eyes were the young eyes of children
looking at their mother, that she will explain.

What were the reasons?   Power of a man over
a woman, his children: his hand on power he lacked,
that my womb had made children as the eye makes a look.

What were the reasons?   Terror of a man left alone,
the terror at a gesture: my hand sliding from her
soft pulse neck, to jawbone, chin, mouth met,
mouth of sharp salt.   We walked the barrier island,
us, the two boys, the skittering orange crabs,
public deserted beach.   In front of the children.

The danger: eyes taught not to cringe away,
the power of their eyes drawn to our joined hands.

Filthy, unfit, not to touch:
                    those from my womb,
red birthslime, come by my cry of agony and pleasure.

Hands smeared often enough with their shit, vomit,
blackness of dirt and new blood, but water from my hands,
and in them, weight of their new bodies come back to rest.

When behind the closed eyelid of a door, in the heavy bed,
sweaty, salty, frantic and calling out sublimely
another woman's name, hands unclenched, I brought down
a cry of joy, then my mouth, mind, hands became
not fit to touch.

                    The work is the same.

What are the reasons?   I told them these.
They were young, they did not understand.
Nor do I.   Words heard in the ear, hollow room.
The eye waits, sad, unsatisfied,
to embrace the particular loved shape.
Eyes, empty   hands, empty   waiting.

Sounds from My Previous Life

The jackhammer, a woodpecker
early in the morning.   The bus
troubling up 8th Street, rain coming
back.   Sounds from my previous life.

Late at night my womb cramps up
like a knotted leg muscle after a run.
There seems no reason for this pain
vibrating in my belly, a rung bell.

Not my time of the month, but 1:00 A.M.
by the dim moon of the electric clock,
the night time fourteen years ago
when I began my second labor.

Not done yet: my body struck
by its life, clapper in a brass bell.

Down the Little Cahaba

Soundless sun, the river.   Home in August
we float down the Little Cahaba, the three of us,
rubber inner tubes, hot laps, in water so slow
we hear the rapids moving upstream toward us,
the whispers coming loud.
                    Then the river bends,
the standing water at the lip, hover, hover,
the moment before orgasm, before the head emerges,
then over suddenly, and sound rushing
back from my ears.
                    The youngest caught in the rapids:
half-grown, he hasn't lived with me in years,
yet his head submerged at a scrape of rock pushes
pain through me, a streak inside my thighs,
vagina to knee.
                    Swept to the outside curve,
the boys climb upstream to plunge down again.

I stand at the mud bank to pick up
shells, river mussels with iridescent inner skin,
with riverine scars from once-close flesh.

    Years back, at the beach, with piles of shells
    in our laps, with the first final separation on us,
    one asked: *How do we know you won't forget us?*

    I told them how they had moved in my womb: each
    distinct, the impatient older, the steady younger.
    I said: *I can never forget you.   You moved inside me.*

I meant: *The sound of your blood crossed into mine.*

The Child Taken from the Mother

I could do nothing.   Nothing.   Do you
understand?   Women ask: *Why didn't you—?*
like they do of women who've been raped.
And I ask myself: Why didn't I?   Why
didn't I run away with them?   Or face
him in court?   Or—

                              Ten years ago I
answered myself: No way for children to live.
Or: The chance of absolute loss.   Or:

I did the best I could.   It was not
enough.   It was about terror and power.
I did everything I could.   Not enough.

This is not the voice of the guilty mother.

Clumsy with anger even now, it is a voice
from the woman shoved outside, one night, as words
clack into place like bricks, poker chips.

A man mutters: *It's a card game.   Too
candid.   They know what's in your hand.*
I look down.   My hands dangle open and empty
in the harsh yellow light.   Strange men,
familiar, laugh and curse in the kitchen, whiskey,
bending over cards.   Or is it something held down
on the table?   Someone says: *Bull Dog Bend.*
Someone says: *The place of the father in the home.*

A woman's voice: *Those women who've never held*
a little baby in their arms. In the old window,
a shadow. Two hands, brick and mortar, seal
the house, my children somewhere inside. The youngest
has lost his baby fat, navel flattened, last
of my stomach's nourishing.

You say: *Do something.*
You say: *Why is this happening?*

My body. My womb.
My body of a woman, a mother, a lesbian.

And here,
perhaps, you say: *That last word doesn't belong.*
Woman, mother: those can stay. Lesbian: no.
Put that outside the place of the poem. Too
slangy, prosy, obvious, just doesn't belong.
Why don't you—? Why didn't you—? Can't you
say it some other way?

The beautiful place
we stood arguing, after the movie, under blue-white
fluorescence. Two middle-aged women in jeans,
two grown boys, the lanky one, the tactful one,
bundled in a pause before cold outside, to argue
the significances: bloody birth, the man cursing
a woman in the kitchen, dirt, prayer, the place
of the father, the master, the beatings, black and
white, home lost, continents, two women
lovers glimpsed, the child taken from the mother
who returns.

No one says: This is about us.   But
in the narrow corridor, stark cement block walls,
we become huge, holding up the harsh images,
the four of us loud, familiar.

                                    Other movie-
goers squeeze past, light their cigarettes,
glance, do not say even to themselves: Children
and women, lovers, mothers, lesbians.   Yes.

All the Women Caught in Flaring Light

1.

A grey day, drenched, humid, the sun-
flowers bowed with rain.   I walk aimless
to think about this poem.   Clear water runs
as if in a streambed, middle of the alley,
a ripple over bricks and sandy residue,
for a few feet pristine as a little creek
in some bottomland, but then I corner
into the dumped trash, mattresses, a stew
of old clothes.   I pull out a wooden fold-up
chair, red vinyl seat, useful for my room,
while water seeps into my shoes.   A day to
be inside, cozy.   Well, let's pick a room:

Imagine a big room of women doing anything,
playing cards, having a meeting, the rattle
of paper or coffee cups or chairs pushed back,
the loud and quiet murmur of their voices,
women leaning their heads together.   If we
leaned in at the door and I said, *Those women
are mothers*, you wouldn't be surprised, except
at me for pointing out the obvious fact.

Women *are* mothers, aren't they?   So obvious.

Say we walked around to 8th or 11th Street
to drop in on a roomful of women, smiling, intense,
playing pool, the green baize like moss.   One
lights another's cigarette, oblique glance.
Others dance by twos under twirling silver moons
that rain light down in glittering drops.
If I said in your ear, through metallic guitars,
These women are mothers, you wouldn't believe me,
would you?   Not really, not even if you had come
to be one of the women in that room.   You'd say:
Well, maybe, one or two, a few.   It's what we say.

Here, we hardly call our children's names out loud.
We've lost them once, or fear we may.   We're careful
what we say.   In the clanging silence, pain falls
on our hearts, year in and out, like water cutting
a groove in stone, seeking a channel, a way out,
pain running like water through the glittering room.

2.

I often think of a poem as a door that opens
into a room where I want to go.   But to go in

here is to enter where my own suffering exists
as an almost unheard low note in the music,
amplified, almost unbearable, by the presence
of us all, reverberant pain, circular, endless,

which we speak of hardly at all, unless a woman
in the dim privacy tells me a story of her child
lost, now or twenty years ago, her words sliding
like a snapshot out of her billfold, faded outline
glanced at and away from, the story elliptic, oblique
to avoid the dangers of grief.   The flashes of story
brilliant and grim as strobe lights in the dark,
the dance shown as grimace, head thrown back in pain.

Edie's hands, tendons tense as wire, spread, beseeched,
how she'd raised them, seven years, and now not even
a visit, Martha said she'd never see the baby again,
her skinny brown arms folded against her flat breasts,
flat-assed in blue jeans, a dyke looking hard as a hammer:
And who would call her a mother?
                                                      Or tall pale Connie,
rainbow skirts twirling, her sailing-away plans, islands,
women plaiting straw with shells: Who would have known
until the night, head down on my shoulder, she cried out
for her children shoved behind the father, shadows
who heard him curse her from the door, hell's fire
as she waited for them in the shriveled yard?

All the women caught in flaring light, glimpsed
in mystery: The red-lipped, red-fingertipped woman
who dances by, sparkling like fire, is she here on the sly,
four girls and a husband she'll never leave from fear?
The butch in black denim, elegant as ashes, her son
perhaps sent back, a winter of no heat, a woman's salary.
The quiet woman drinking gin, thinking of being sixteen,
the baby wrinkled as wet clothes, seen once, never again.

Loud music, hard to talk, and we're careful what we say.
A few words, some gesture of our hands, some bit of story
cryptic as the mark gleaming on our hands, the ink
tattoo, the sign that admits us to this room, iridescent
in certain kinds of light, then vanishing, invisible.

3.

If suffering were no more than a song's refrain
played through four times with its sad lyric,
only half-heard in the noisy room, then done with,
I could write the poem I imagined: All the women
here see their lost children come into the dim room,
the lights brighten, we are in the happy ending,
no more hiding, we are ourselves and they are here
with us, a reconciliation, a commotion of voices.

I've seen it happen.   I have stories from Carla,
Wanda.   I have my own: the hammering at authority,
the years of driving round and round for a glimpse,
for anything, and finally the child, big, awkward,
comes with you, to walk somewhere arm in arm.

But things have been done to us that can never be
undone.   The woman in the corner smiling at friends,
the one with black hair glinting white, remembers
the brown baby girl's weight relaxed into her lap,
the bottle in her right hand, cigarette in her left,
the older blonde girl pressed tense at her shoulder,
the waves' slap on the rowboat, the way she squinted
as the other woman, her lover, took some snapshots,
the baby sucking and grunting rhythmic as the water.

The brown-eyed baby who flirted before she talked,
taken and sent away twenty years ago, no recourse,
to a tidy man-and-wife to serve as daughter.
If she stood in the door, the woman would not know her,
and the child would have no memory of the woman,
not of lying on her knees nor at her breast, leaving
a hidden mark, pain grooved and etched on the heart.

The woman's told her friends about the baby.   They
keep forgetting.   Her story drifts away like smoke,
like vague words in a song, a paper scrap in the water.
When they talk about mothers, they never think of her.

No easy ending to this pain.   At midnight we go home
to silent houses, or perhaps to clamorous rooms full
of those who are now our family.   Perhaps we sit alone,
heavy with the past, and there are tears running bitter
and steady as rain in the night.   Mostly we just go on.

The Place Lost and Gone, the Place Found

One low yellow light, the back room a cave,
musty sleeping bags, us huddled on the floor.
We pretend we're camped somewhere with no calendar,
distant from morning when I will leave and leave
them motherless children again.   The oldest travels
into sleep, holds my hand while I listen, left,
to a huge wind come up in my hollow ears, my breath,
pain, and me asking: What are we besides this pain,
this frail momentary clasp?
                                               At the window next day
the face of the youngest stiff with grief, and at my desk
beside me years after, his face, clear, fixed,
like a photo set in a paperweight, crystal heavy pain.
Pick it up, unable to put it down.
                                               Yet woven,
still twined in my hand, his sinewy fingers like twigs
in the tree we climbed the first day:
                                               As soon as I jumped
from the car and hugged them, each a small *oomph*,
they rushed me to climb their tree, maple in the jumbled
wild green strip of land between houses and lawns,
up, feet there, there's the nest, rumpled,
suspended.   They long for the hidden bird.   We talk
about what I can't remember, nothing but words.   We drop
seeds into light, translucent silent whirligigs,
better than copters, they say, and gently rock
the branch I sit on with their long scratched legs.

They have asked me into their tree and, satisfied,
we sit rather large in its airy room.   Their house
slides away across the lawn to the edge.   Now
we are in the middle.   Now they show me the inside.

If I see a small grass motion, it's probably voles.
That muddy excavation will be dug bigger, longer,
for a cave, for a hideout with a tin roof.   And all
paths, distinct or vague in the rank weeds, go
places.   The oldest leads me to his, a pond
sunk, hedged, and forgotten.   No one else comes.
He watches in the morning (silver), in the evening (gold).
For what?   For the birds, to be the one who sees
and takes the bird away, but only with his eyes.

The youngest boy takes me to the smallest creek.
We see the crawfish towers squiggled in the mud.
We see dim passageways down to hidden creatures,
mysteries.   We follow scarce water under a road
into sun.   They show me jewelweed, touch-me-not,
dangling red-orange tiny ears, and the brown pods,
how seed rattles and springs and scatters if you fling
out your hand, even carelessly.   They show me everything,
saying, with no words, they have thought of me here,
and here I am with them in the in-between places.

A Waving Hand

Last night of the visit, the youngest put his head
down, saying, *Again and again and again and again
and again,* his head down on the bed.
                                        I said
we should get a medal for every time we say good-bye,
like a purple heart; or we could have a waving hand
(*Like the one in the windows of roaring trucks,*
he says).
                    Our chests would be heavy with
medals, heavy waving hands: pendulum:

we come back, we say hello.   He cheered up, then.

Seven Times Going, Seven Coming Back

I said I would not be a tragedy.
I said to myself: *Life, life,*

life, as if keeping time with my feet,
as if marching.   Sometimes I heard: *Stupid,*

stupid, days when every thought was a blow
to my heart, though not a mark on me,

not a sign of what had left me stumbling
in the streets, mumbling like a shell-shocked

woman in a photograph of war, dead baby
in her shawl, the crumpled ruined walls.

Then I would think: How serious is
the fate of one woman standing dazed,

alone by a wire fence, staring at red
camellias, thinking of her children carried

away by their father as if captured,
as if to another country?   Only I was saying

tragedy.   No one else saw.   No one
tracked me with a helicopter to take pictures

as I drove over the grey smoke mountains,
crossed the Pigeon River seven

times going, seven coming back.
Ice latticed the wall of rock,

ice cleaved the rock, water cleft.
When I left, no one heard me, keening

my children.
                            But in tragedy you don't know
why, and I knew the father, and the law

over me.   To be closed, alone,
in an underground room or cave, the opening

a blur of sun.   To watch as shadow hands
lay stone, to watch the light vanish

granite rock by rock.   The woman who defied
her fate, who also said: *I choose death.*

What is tragedy?   To believe I deserved
judgments implacable as gods on my heart.

Buried alive in my body, room of shame.
For this I failed them, for this I lost them.

My body as the place of loss.   The effort
to say *yes,* to hold my lover's

weight against my breast, and feel the slender
shape of the child taken, and still ask.

The effort to say: *If taken beyond my hands,
almost as if dead, not by me.   I will have my own.*

A darkened room.   Color film stutters
on the screen.   We watch a crowd falter

and surge at crossroads, demanding water.
A dark woman talks about her children.   We hear

the parched land, the deaths, the miles.
She sits locked in barracks, steel,

not prison, off-hours from a company job.
No children allowed, just hot plates, cots.

A friend brings the children to her.   At the gate
no one in or out.   Guards see to that.

She reaches her hands to them through the fence,
through an iron grill, to the heads of her children.

In the dark I pray to somebody (is it myself?)
who will not divide self from self, self from life.

Shame

1.

I ask for justice but do not release
myself.   Do I think I was wrong?   Yes.
Of course.   Was wrong.   Am wrong.   Can
justify everything except their pain.
Even now their cries rattle in my ears
like icy winds pierce in cold weather.
Even now a tenderness from their cries.

The past repeats in fragments: What I
see is everybody watching, me included,
as a selfish woman leaves her children,
two small boys hardly more than babies.

Though I say he took them, and my theories
explain power, how he thought he'd force
me to choose, me or them, her or them.

2.

How I wanted her slant humid body,
that first woman, silent reach,
how I began with her furtive mouth,
her silences, her hand fucking me
back of the van, beach sand grit
scritch at my jeans, low tide.

　　The boys yelling in myrtle thickets
　　outside, hurl pell-mell, count hide-
　　and-seek.　The youngest opens the door.
　　What I am doing is escape into clouds,
　　grey heat, promise of thunderstorm
　　not ominous, not sordid, from ground
　　to air, like us flying kites in March.
　　But here it's July and I'm doing what?

Curious, left out, he tells some fragment later
to the father, who already knows.　The threats
get worse, spat curses:　He'll take the children;
I can go fly where I damn please in the world.
The muttered words for scum, something rotten,
flies buzzing, futile, mean.

　　　　　　　　If I had been
more ashamed, if I had not wanted the world.
If I had hid my lust, I might not have lost
them.　This is where the shame starts.

If I had not been so starved, if I had been
more ashamed and hid.　No end to this blame.

3.

At times I can say it was good, even better
for them, my hunger for her.   Now that we're
here, they've grown up, survived, no suicides,
despite their talk of walks in front of cars,
smashing through plate glass.   Despite guilt:

> The long sweating calls to the twelve-year-
> old, saying, *Hold on* against the pain,
> how I knew it from when I left, the blame
> inside, the splintered self, saying to him, *Walk
> out*, remind the body you are alive, even if
> rain is freezing in the thickets to clatter
> like icy seeds, even if you are the only one
> plodding through the drifts of grainy snow.

Now we've survived.   They call to talk poetry
or chaos of physics.   Out of the blue to hear
their voices, a kind of forgiveness, a giddy
lifting of my heart:
> Like the kites we flew once
> below the Occoneechee Mountain, down in the pasture.
> The wind spirited our plastic birds, hawks, eagles,
> or crumpled them while we shouted, *No, no*.   I waded
> deep into the blackberry thicket thorns for the miracle
> wings that soon we made disappear again like airplanes,
> soon made to come back from mystery travels:

The way the boys appear today in my city, old enough to
come by rackety plane or train, whiz in to be
with me, my lover now, eat spaghetti, talk serious
politics in my kitchen, snug, but a feeling of travel.

Their curious eyes are on life that widens in a place
little known, our pleasure without shame.   We talk
and the walls seem to shift and expand around us.
The breaking of some frozen frame.   The youngest jokes
lovebirds at our held hands.   Late evening we stir.
Goodnight: they expect me to go off to bed with her.

4.

All the years between now and then, the nights.
One December when I thought she would leave me,
was weeping her hand's loss, her body's weight

lifting away, and thought: I will lose her
like I lost the children.   I will lose her.
And knew my body's secret thought, endured

as a voice creeping on my skin, a buzz,
a sandfly's bite of pain, a grain of sand
caught in the sheets, abrading my skin.   *Loss,*

said the voice, *love is loss.*   Don't forget
the children, how pleasure brings pain.
Don't forget you're to blame.   Don't forget

how pain digs in your hands, like thorns stuck
and broken off, invisible ache you feel
whenever you touch.   You lose what you touch.

You've learned it.   Don't want too much.
Think of her arms as nothing: blowing foam,
drifting cloud, scudding caress.

Reality is flesh of your flesh taken.
What you want to last is fantasy, imagination,
said the voice creeping in my body, pain.

5.

In one hand, the memory of pain.
I reread one of these poems and begin
again (again, it's been fifteen years)
to cry at the fragmented naked faces,
at the noise of the crying, somewhere
inside us, even now, like an old wind.
In one hand, the memory of pain.

In the other hand, change.   When
did it begin? Over and over.   Once
we all were walking on the street,
me and her, hand in hand, very loud
singing sixties rock-and-roll, rattle,
shake, smiling goofily, indecent
(but not quite illegally), escaped
out with the boys in a gusty wind.
The youngest sang, the oldest lagged,
ashamed?   But we waited for him.
It was a comedy, a happy ending,
pleasure.   We kept saying, *Spring,
it's spring,* so the boys brought us
to their lake, its body-thick ice thinned
at the edge to broken glass splinters.
The new waves widened and glittered in the ice,
a delicate clinking like glass wind chimes.

And now, sometimes, one of them will say: *Remember
the day we all went down to the lake?   Remember
how we heard the sound of the last ice in the water?*

Motionless on the Dark Side of the Light

When I try to get back to my mother
at first I don't want to see the child
on her knees by the bed who is praying
against her hands, face and hands placed
flat and cool on the rough blue-and-white
woven bedspread that burns wet, hot, wet
after a while in the half-darkness.   Light
slices by her from the cracked kitchen
door, voices fall through into her room.

Motionless on the dark side of the light,
she kneels and listens to her mother talk
to her father, her mother's voice slurred,
desperate, a voice she's never heard before.
His reeks of whiskey, pills, death.   Reckless,
the mother threatens to kill herself too.
Is that what he wants?   In the lighted room
one of them decides.   All the child can do is pray.
Her knees hurt from the rug, nubby as gravel.
She prays her mother will not leave her.
She prays in the dark room rimmed with light.
She prays to someone there, but who is there?
Does she ask out loud?   Does she ask, silent?

The white fluorescence by her slowly widens.
Her mother has come to ask why she is crying.
Her mother says she will stay, promises to live.

The child begins to pray nights by the window.
Some nights the moon opens its full mouth and
takes her   silently kneeling   inside   fearless.

The Mother Before Memory

1.

Enormous mythic figures shine in a silent dark,
the mother with child at her breast, her knee.

Photographs flash past like an art history
lecture, but with no blue-cloaked white Virgin,
no black vulture-winged, horn-crowned Isis
hiding the tiny boy god. Instead there I am,
the child, ringletted, lace-collar smock, white
on white skin, leaning against the black mother,
massive, enigmatic, weighty hat, dark clothes.
Both stare unsmiling at the camera. Who paid
for this picture? What did they want remembered?

Long years after, what does the child think,
looking at the picture? In my hands it would bend:
soft pasteboard, sepia, antique, shocking
proof of time when it was us only, the two of us.
(Does the child say *my black mother?*) I have a picture
of her holding me in her arms, up in the sunlight.
She is in headrag and sagging apron. The backyard,
the scuppernong vine shadow. 1946. I am a baby.
It is a breath of time in the years she held me.

2.

Pictures somewhere, in a cardboard candy box,
my mother holding me. (Does the child say
my white mother?) What I remember is a story:
how those years before memory I never cried.
She squatted by me, tried an even, reasoned voice.
I never cried. No memory of her mouth, her face.

I remember lying by her, massive in the dark,
the slow beating of her voice through hymns,
through last century's love songs, and I slept.

I remember her proud silence. But somewhere
her voice talks to her self in me. Somewhere
in me a voice like our church bell that rang
once a week only: the harsh repeated metal clang,
outcry in silence. Her voice praying in me.

3.

No story, no picture of the first memory,
what I'm not supposed to remember: being held
by her, dark in a darkening room, face unseen,
but it is her. I am safe. I never called her
my mother. I am in her lap, warm, surrounded.
We are floating in humid air. All the windows
open. The katydids drone, bend, then louder.
The summer air vibrates like a drum: we are
inside some huge long song of anticipation.
Darkness and sound are outside and in us.

4.

A kodacolor snapshot: the boys, her,
and me against the unpainted board walls.
Behind us a yellow paper calendar fades.
I am grown up.   She is shrunken and smudged.
Stifling heat in her old box of a room.
Coals burn, cry, crumble in the iron stove.

She nods at how I answer her questions:
I left the man; he got the children.
She inclines her head to signify us two
in the long story of women and children
severed.   With a nod she declares us
not guilty, and begins to give advice.

Her sibilant words I scarcely understand,
delta language, her a child on a plantation
talking to her own people, Mr. John Ed's land.
(Did she talk to the child before memory?
Did the child understand?)   What I hear is
the slash of machete on cane, a heavy sack
dragging through sand, the thud of a gun,
dead bone at the spine, and a voice crying.
Her children cry out to her, but which ones?

The words I salvage are few, fierce, clear:
Bind them to you, bind them while you can.

5.

On the bright white wall of my room
a pen-and-ink sketch on yellow paper,
an old woman, the black goddess of Ephesus,
the mother with a thousand drooping breasts.

A picture hung there by my need for someone
bigger than me to pray to.   What would I ask
the black mother, cool shadow refuge in the heat;
the white mother, moon's logic in the night?
One is dead, one lives on in silent need.

Nothing to do but strike a match, put a light
nodding on the candle.   Stand at the scattered
objects of my life: pictures, a ring, a bell,
a jar of red clay, little tongues of leaves,
a boll of cotton brought from home, open
black calyx edged like a whetted knife,
the dusty cotton soft and worn as a breast.

Ring the bell, small brass call.   Pray to them
in me, and for what they gave, before memory.

Two Small-Sized Girls

1.

Two small-sized girls, hunched in the corn crib,
skin prickly with heat and dust.   We rustle
in the corn husks and grab rough cobs gnawed
empty as bone.   We twist them with papery shreds.
Anyone passing would say we're making our dolls.

Almost sisters, like our mothers, we turn and shake
the shriveled beings.   We are not playing at babies.
We are doing, single-minded, what we've been watching
our grandmother do.   We are making someone.   We hunker
on splintered grey planks older than our mothers,
and ignore how the sun blazes across us, the straw husks,
the old door swung open for the new corn of the summer.

2.

Here's the cherry spool bed from her old room,
the white bedspread crocheted by Grandma,
rough straw baskets hanging on the blank wall,
snapshots from her last trip home, ramshackle
houses eaten up by kudzu.   The same past
haunts us.   We have ended up in the same present

where I sit crosslegged with advice on how to keep
her children from being seized by their father
ten years after I lost my own.   The charge then:
crime against nature, going too far with women,
and not going back to men.   And hers?   Wanting
to have her small garden the way she wanted it,
and wanting to go her own way.   The memory:

    Her father's garden, immense rows of corn,
    cantaloupe and melon squiggling, us squatting,
    late afternoon, cool in the four o'clocks,
    waiting for them to open, making up stories,
    anything might happen, waiting in the garden.

3.

So much for the power of my ideas about oppression
and her disinterest in them.   In fact we've ended
in the same place.   Made wrong, knowing we've done
nothing wrong:
                    Like the afternoon we burned up
the backyard, wanting to see some fire.
The match's seed opened into straw, paper,
then bushes, like enormous red and orange
lantana flowers.   We chased the abrupt power
blooming around us down to charred straw,
and Grandma bathed us, scorched and ashy,
never saying a word.

                    Despite our raw hearts,
guilt from men who used our going to take our children,
we know we've done nothing wrong, to twist and search
for the kernels of fire deep in the body's shaken husk.

The First Question

The first question is: *What do your children*
think of you?   No interest in the kudzu-green
burial of the first house I lived in,

nor in the whiskey, the heat, or the people sweating
in church under huge rotate hands in the ceiling.
The question is never the Selma march, and me

breathing within thirty miles, or the sequence
of Dante, five poems, a husband, two children,
no poems, pregnancy and the concept of women's

liberation, or how the rain was slick and warm
on my mouth on her mouth, or why poetry returned.
And, yes, I give a different life's version

each time, but no matter what panorama veers
and recedes on the blackboard, white wall, behind me,
someone chooses my two boys to face me:

accusers, opponents, judges?   Then I tell a joke,
and never tell of the long nights I choked
on my own questions.

                    And never tell anyone, only we
remember:

The long drive home, live heat

changed at midnight speed to wind,
our mouths singing, drinking the humid
cool breath of trees, and yelling swift

blackness to come home with us, reckless
in the deep night, carrying everything with us,
all life and even death without a pause before us,

the sudden red-eyed possum, live eyes
dead, impossible but gone, our cries,
grief, and them questioning me, miles,

or perhaps this happened after the curve
we hurtled and the moon, huger than a world
directly in the road, moved our moves,

low orange eye, high hot-white when we got home.
They were nine and ten, one moment
out of years, except years after, the oldest

takes me up the stairs to show
his first painting, acrylic oil blue-
black sky barely edging around a moon.

Enormous memory   child mother moon   orange moon.

My Life You Are Talking About

The ugliness, the stupid repetition
when I mention my children, or these poems,
or myself as mother.   My anger when someone
tries to make my life into a copy of
an idea in her head, flat, paper thin.

How can I make any of this into a poem?
What do I mean by *this?*   For instance:

Me standing by the xerox machine, clack, slide, whish.   Another
teacher, I've known her for five years, asks what I've been writing,
lately,

and I say: *These poems about my children,*

holding up the pages.   Her face blanks.   I'd never seen that
happen, the expression, a blank face—vacant, emptied.

She says: *I didn't know you had children.*

So I say: *That's what these are about.   Not many people know
I have children.   They were taken away from me.*

She says: *You're kidding.*

I say: *No, I'm not kidding.   I lost my children because I'm
a lesbian.*

She says: *But how could that happen to someone with a Ph.D.?*

I lean against a desk.   I want to slap her with anger.

Instead,
I answer: *I'm a pervert, a deviant, low as someone on the street,*
              as a prostitute, a whore.   I'm unnatural, queer.   I'm a
              lesbian.   I'm not fit to have children.

I didn't
explain: A woman who's loose with men is trash; a woman
              with a woman is to be punished.

Because this woman was supposed to be a feminist and
understand something.

I walk away, carrying off the poems,
useless words, black tracks on flimsy paper.
So much for the carry-over of metaphor
and the cunning indirection of the poet (me)

who lures the listener (her) deeper and deeper
with bright images, through thorns, a thicket,
into a hidden openness (the place beyond the self:
see any of the preceding or following poems).

So much for the imagination.   I don't say:
You've known for years who I am.   Have you
never imagined what happened to me day
in and out, out in your damned straight world?

Why give her a poem to use to follow me
as I gather up the torn bits, a path made
of my own body, a trail to find
what has been lost, what has been taken,

when, if I stand in the room, breathing,
sweating a little, with a shaky voice,
blood-and-bones who tells what happened,
I get her disbelief?   Or worse:

A baby-faced lesbian, her new baby snug in her closed arms,
smiles, matronizing, smug, and asks had I ever thought of
having children?

Have you ever thought of having children?

What I thought as the pay-phone
doctor's voice pronounced jovial
stunning pregnancy, advised philosophy
(why he had five, this one's only my
second) was: Where would my life be
in this concept *mother-of-two?*
There was no one around to see.
I could cry all I wanted while
I sat down and got used to the idea.

At a friend's house for dinner, we talk about my boys, her
girl, the love affairs of others, how I like morning bed with
my lover.   She complains how sex is hard to get with a three-
year-old around, glances at me as if to say: You have it so
easy.   Does say:

Well, if you had children.

In his crib the first baby bangs
his head on the side, little worm
wailing lost earth.   He burrows,
pushes through, in, out my vagina,
while in another room, I cringe
at the push of his father's penis.

Other side of the door, the two boys
half-grown, rest gangly in their sleep.
In bed, her hand slides, cold, doubtful
from my breast.   She frets: *What are they
thinking?*   While I whisper, hot, heat
in my breath, how I lost them for touch,
dangerous touch, and we would not believe
the mean knifing voice that says we lose
every love if we touch.   We pull close,
belly to belly, kiss, push, push,
no thought in writhe against ache,
our sweaty skin like muddy ground
when we come back to being there in bed,
and to the sleeping presence of children.

In a classroom, we wind through ideas about women, power,
the loss of children, men and ownership, the loss of self,
the lesbian mother.   They have heard me tell how it has been
for me.   The woman to my left, within hand's reach, never
turns her face toward me.   But speaks about me:

It's just not good for children to be in that kind of home.

I am stripped, naked, whipped.
Splintered by anger, wordless.
I want to break her, slash her.
My edged eyes avoid her face.

I say: *Why do you think this?*

I do not say: What have you lost?   What have you ever
                lost?

Later I say: *This is my life you are talking about.*

She says: *I didn't mean it personally.*

Over the phone, someone I've known for years asks what am I
writing now?

I say: *I'm working hard on some poems about my
                children.*

She says: Oh, how sweet.   How sweet.

I Am Ready to Tell All I Know

From the North (where cold white is falling
now) he says: *We are learning about the South,
in History.   Terrible things have happened there.*

From the South (the edge, but roses are opening
their red mouths here, in November) I say:
Yes.

I am ready to tell more.   I am ready to
tell him all I know.   He says: *Let's don't
get into it now.*

He is fifteen.   He says if he thinks about
it, he can't live every day: his math,
and rowing the red lake water at dawn.

I think of how I lost him as a child
when no one, there, would speak for me
because I was *it*.

His tender neck lost to my mouth, and his brother
only a terrible absent weight in my arms, every day,
because my love inverted history.

I think about how terrible things
continue.   At nineteen what did Michael
Donald think as they strangled him,

before he died in their ropey noose
hung from a small camphor tree,
black, in a cluttered empty lot in Mobile?

He fought them, he fought them.
The men returned to their card-playing friends,
soaked through clothes to white skin with blood.

When my children bleed, my own blood rushes
as if out of me.   What if he were one of mine?
But which bloodied one, mine?

In the Waiting Room at the Draft Board

He called me the day after we invaded
Grenada.   Low green hills exploded
into rock, flesh, people's bones.
I am ashamed of this country, he said.

Once he was a sack of living bones
I hauled.   I pushed the heavy belly
uphill, months of summer and green war
in Vietnam.   I sat down one afternoon,
lap full of silent weight.   I sat
waiting on a narrow metal chair, cold
tin through thin cloth, my thighs
split, dull ache in my cunt.   Waiting
for a uniformed man to come take a look:

   The father offers me as a piece of evidence.
   Clear to see: My flesh is the field, spread,
   plowed, and now the fruit, the root crop.
   Here is the land that needs its farmer.
   Here is the country that needs its ruler.
   Here is the child that needs its father.
   Let him stay at home and not go to war.

I push my stomach out, weight drags
my back.   The man talks and stares at
a thin swollen white girl, almost a mother,
my belly cut by his eyes.   Exactly what is
there?   Is it enough?   Will it buy freedom?

Grown, he's asking questions about his father:
Was he an innocent man, victim, pushed
aside for my freedom?   I retell what I've told
before: He was a man who escaped the war,
but when I left, he seized both children.

Maybe I don't mention the legal terror,
the threat letters: *Her unorthodox ideas*
about men and the father in the home.   But
I'm clear about how the father was not god.
I'd seen his front, and his backside too.

I don't use these words exactly.   I don't
throw rocks at his father.   I tell stories
about how I fought him, some funny.   We laugh,
lighter, as if stones have fallen out of us.
I don't know where he is bruised from when
I paid for my freedom with my children.

While Reading Timerman's *The Longest War*

The father who says to the son: *It is time*
to rebel, but do not leave alone.   Talk
to the others.
                    And do not go to Lebanon
where

cluster bombs

women raped with broken bottles

Yes, yes, the voice of the father.   They
will listen to him, as never to the voice
of the mother: whining, complaining, un-
realistic, hysterical, irrational, my
voice
            our voices, saying over and over,
Don't do it, don't go.

Some of us saying this, others saying, *Go.*

But never, almost never, the voice of the father
saying: *Don't go*
                    to Grenada where
                    to Lebanon where
                    to Nicaragua, Honduras, Guatemala

where

At the Vietnam Memorial

A black wall, grass rooting on top, sod over a grave, a mirror,
a bank of black clay, a granite gravestone with names, 50,000,
gritblasted, almost all men, names, sons of some mother.

I shimmer in the wall like a ghost in a dimension of death.

The other tourists rush around me, people with ice-cream cones,
bicycles, with baby carriages, with metal taps in their shoes because
they are Marines;
       people leaving white peonies, carnations, roses
dyed black, stuck in the cracks of the wall,

            leaving propped
in the dirt an engraved announcement, an Episcopalian funeral,

leaving taped to the granite a newsclipping, death by land-mine;

the people leaving *yahrzeit* candles, burning shimmering flames;

the people with their heads propped against the wall, looking
for the one name;
       the people who have left behind letters
wrapped in plastic baggies against the rain.
          I find a letter
that's been left for me, from a mother to her dead son:
how on the dead wall she has just read his name, the one
she gave him when she held him the hour after birth.

How am I to answer this letter?

Dear mother of a dead son:

I have two sons, and I am afraid that, as with yours, so with mine:

that the two wings of this death bird   the two arms of this grave will meet around them:

and their names that have rolled out of my mouth like peonies, like the tapping sound of woodpeckers:

that the sound of their names will one day be nothing but grit-blasted marks on a wall propping up the dirt, their rotting bodies.

Talking to Charlie

The cafeteria.   Women, and alone, an eighteen-year-old
boy eating breakfast, diffident mouth, scant food.   School.

I do not have to sit with him, not my child, but I do,
and eat my flat fried egg: cynical eye, yellow crocus
in the snow outside, speaking mouth.   He opens
his mouth.   The words will be: Hate men, don't you?
Last night I'd read a poem out loud: men, rape, the screw-
driver, the woman's eyes.

                    His face convulses red,
muscles of his mouth struggle to push words fleshed
out, a new thing, onto the table between us.   I gave
him something.   He is giving me back a bloody live
making of his own.
                    He says: *The righteous anger of
women, the times I hate myself as a man.   Not
to be.   I get lonely.*

                    His face.   My sons' look at me.

The three of us, faces bright as early suns, grinning,
reflected in the creek's surface, summer.   We wade in,

swim, until four shadow men arrive in the slipping light,
gauge with eyes how close we are until night, nod politely.

We leave.   I rage.   My oldest says: *If you hate
them—men—you hate us.*   My voice answers: *Rape,
history, the grasp of danger.*   My voice splits, frantic
in the tiny car, classroom.   Their faces blank.

At the table Charlie waits for me to answer.   No shadow
faces float in the dull formica.   *I get lonely,* I say.
What will you say to the other men?   And to my sons?

Dreaming a Few Minutes in a Different Element

1.

The boys are running through a blaze of sand.
At my back is the road, rutted, muddy, and the sun
pushing me like a hand in the middle of my back.

Below, the creek, its cool smell rising, animal
scent, promise, the incessant water released,
hidden seeps and springs.   Down I go, big, small,
my tracks, my children's feet.   The tussled sand
covers and uncovers buried outlines, my younger feet
just bigger than a raccoon's, than a bobcat's,
small as my mother's ear, big as her hand, then
big enough so that here at the damp edge, I stand
where everything mingles, simultaneous, undivided
instant before we plunge into the green sliding-
south cold water.

                    In the leap I jump out
from my enormous mother, from her arms, her black suit
cool and rubbery like the floating innertubes, but
her belly big and mine to lean on, watch the water
creviced between her breasts, buoyant because she
floats me, more than we are on land.   She holds me,
safety to my risk, and I leap between water and water,
ecstasy, another being gathered by the light sparkling
into children, mothers, the jagged heights above, flying
air, the long, long slant of sun, afternoon, motionless
time.

Mornings, grown older, I come with the cousins,
no grownups.   The boys dive death-close to limestone
teeth, the green water mouth the mothers warn about.
At noon they swim to the hidden spring, down to the bone-
cold inner underground water.   They grope in and float
out a watermelon, mottled green and white, dark and light,
the world spinning in glossy space in our science text.
The oldest girl splits it for us with a butcher knife:
the slow cracking breaks open suddenly to red delicate flesh.

Behind me in the sand, melon rind sticks up, dry rib.
Alongside, seeds sprout double green leaves, sib
to drops of blood, a green row repeating like a heartbeat.

We are swimming in the creek, the boys and I, afloat,
hands hovered in figure eights of infinity,
in water steady as our blood, but cold, and older.

2.

I have passed through a mean, barren place,
an anti-creek, the opposite of the creek where:

There is no sun, no noon, no sand, no green.
There is dirt, but fired and glazed, a floor
tiled so hard no tracks show.   There is
water, but it is always the same airless water
pumped around, shallow spray, falling, smelling
of chlorine, dead.   It is a place of no feeling.

I stand in the middle of this no place,
night, calling my mother from a pay phone,
alone, a pile of cold change, my back exposed.
I am telling her I want to come home,
me and the boys.   I have left my husband.
I do not want him to come to her house.
I ask her to take me and not him, and she
refuses.   She says: *He's been like a son to me.*

Now, when I think back, I could say I twisted
the phone line in my hand like an umbilical plastic
cord, or some other metaphor, but I wasn't
thinking then.   In the suburban mall, might as well
have been underground, I was feeling dead,
stood with the back of my head sheared off, the way
quartz rock fractures when hammered, in a cavity
underground, water somewhere, tears, shale.

Stopped.   Eyes shut.   No where to go back to.
My mother says he can bring the boys home.
She gives them to him.   I called, I asked her.
She said: *No.*   She means: *No daughter of mine.*
Wordlessly, she's trying to make me change
back.   Then she would take me back.   Now I am
inhuman, perhaps: half-bear, half-cat or possum,
altered by unnatural sex.   I wander through the shoppers,
wonder what they see: monster, mischance?
If asked, they'd likely say, *You had a choice.*

So did she.   I have reasons for her.   Not one fits
as a key in a lock to open us out of the present.
I'm being childish, yes.   The child doesn't care
why, knows only the mother is not there.

3.

I call my children.   The phone rings, rings.
Its sharp tone rises, vanishes, in a distant place.
A bitter hating voice, then their voices.   They want
to know why I'm not with them.   I listen.   My tongue
gropes, hesitant, in my mouth.   How to explain
a kind of doubling back to myself, selfish or
the difference between the stale fountain I stare at,
and the creek, pure unknown upwelling, sex, what
I put my hands in, how it was to touch her,
like me running down to be the first to meet,
enter, and be taken by the creek in the early morning.

What did this mean to them on unforgiving nights
when they cried out and I was not there to answer?

4.

The boys are swimming the green creek,
time creviced between sand and limestone.
Upstream a moccasin sleeps extended in sun,
doubling a dead branch over water.   Below
it floats redoubled, drowsing, suspended.
The creek comes down in snaky rapids,
huge muscles, ripples over rib bones.

I've swum the boys past the hidden rocks
sharp as a bite or a broken bottle, shown
where the snakes do and do not hole up.
I laze in the heat, skin sand-crinkled.
They dive down just where I dived out
from my mother.   Their father can't give
this, I think, as a blue-tailed, yellow-
lined, orange-headed skink runs at my foot.
Then they come up in a screaming fight,
nothing new, what the boys always do.
Once the mothers made them go upstream alone.
What to do with mine?   Throwing wet
volleys of sand.   What are we back to?

Beer cans piled in the gully, old chlorox
bottles, mottled plastic.   A dirty hot
backwoods swimming hole, narrow
enough to cross in two strokes, I go on,
bitter, to myself, but have to stop,
to stop their fight.   The smallest is
getting the worst of it, of course.

I wade in, break the green opaque surface
into dull glass fragments, sharply cold,
and show them what I used to do: Submerge,
and use the green underwater like a lens,
open the eyes, looking for what is there,
dreaming a few minutes in a different element.

The faint streak of little fish, the dim bottom
rocks heavy with quartz.   Our fingers grope,
sift sand, brittle mussel shells.   We can drift
close to the place where air, land, water meet,
edge of the creek, and see on the damp margin
a squiggled trail, infinite small snail tracks,
no beginning or end, wrinkled, undeciphered,
a message left for us, mysterious words seen
through the huge eye of the creek.
                                                    And the water
pulls at our feet, trying to carry us south,
south, going to the Gulf, going to be sucked up
by clouds or a cyclonic mouth, water floated on
by fishermen, and swum in by beautiful unseen fishes
the color of glass jewels, rose-red, yellow,
iridescent blue and green.   The men haul them out,
year after year seeing a dull spill of thousands,
plain fish, grey in the air, the men unaware
that they were brilliant, different, in another element.

Another Question

1.

Yes, they've seen these poems.   The oldest says
nothing, yet.   It's his voice I've answered
in them, often, since the night he asked about me
and his father, *How did that happen?*   I tell
the sorry story again, to him, a grown-up man:

> His words slide stone from the cave's mouth,
> and we enter together to ask and answer
> questions never voiced before.   A chill,
> a crinkle of skin, as we advance into a place
> unknown, toward the oracle of ourselves.

Now he visits, we talk, go do strange things:
In the backyard, a heavy rain one night.
We squat by the garden in the porch light's sun
to watch the earthworms rise, writhe, huge
as monsters in a tiny odyssey.   We lean over
and, like gods, admire the fabulous worms.

2.

The youngest son is debonair, modern,
reads Yeats, loves political words.

I pick him up from a summer job, midnight
in the steam heat of hot asphalt and the public
fountain.   He's reading in the aqueous light,
gives me a dreamy traveling smile from a place
where he plots a clever footing of words.

One morning he reads my poems, serious,
and says he likes best what he remembers
being in (perhaps like this one.) And also
that I get in the middle and tell it all,
grab people and tell them, just say it.

Yes, they've seen the poems.   The world prefers
I not tell the children: hide, be oblique, be
secret, be grotesque.   But the youngest says
when I tell it all, that's what he likes best.

The Laughing Place

There was the time I got mad and hired a detective,
I told the oldest boy one night he asked for more
stories.   The cluttered supper table rattled and shook
like a car in low gear as he teetered back his chair:

It was spring after the fall I left your father,
and you, in the old brick house with the weedy yard.
He was after me, threats like boots and knives:
Sign the papers or never see your children again.
I was rabbit-scared foolish as if I'd slipped the pen
and, lolloping toward the bushes, heard the man's hands
about to snatch me by my hind legs up and skin me alive.

All spring I was in a sorry crouch, shank-shaking,
waiting.   Maybe he'd get tired of whack, whack
at such stupid red-eyed game.   I went and came
back for nervous visits, sprung free a bit by quick
tizzies of wind investigating the leaves that proved

summer.   Then one day your brother, smooth-cheeked
innocent, crow-eyed, told me about the strange woman
sleeping cozy overnight like a plump feather pillow
in his father's bed.   At first I was just aggravated,

and then, then, I got light-headed, hot-fingered mad at
this young Mr. Buck, laying down the law, do-as-I-say-
not-as-I-do two-faced deceitful man out to lambast
me for doing what I please, doing as he does but with a
different woman.   That's how I got hissing mad as a cat

and called the detective up out of the yellow phonebook
into the snackbar red vinyl booth, a little slick-haired
weasel-worded gold-toothed man, *yes ma'm, no ma'm,*
in his lime polyester suit, green as slime, his promise
of a trail, a furtive gleam at the lit, lidded windows
of the house I later imagined him snoozing in front of,
easy in his rusty Chevy as a mole deep in his hole,
asleep in an earth of dirt, and not a speck of evidence,
mud or rock, to throw, nothing out of him for my money,

except the idea of slinking in dark moonlight to pounce.

So that's what I did, with my lover, in her car.   Sneaked
up the street to lurk and look for any pointed proof
I could use, mean as claws.   We snouted, hooted, prowled
around the house, sniffed, flitted, plotted, but rooted
out only this: a bit of courage in my heart, canny,
cunning, that I could outsmart threat.   Which I did.

I went to the hmmph-hmmphing lawyer and said, *Listen,
I have a story,* told until he slowly picked the phone
up and called the man off me with *Careful, stones, stones
and people in glass houses.*   I'd thought I needed hard
evidence, a rock in the hand.   I'd thought the house
was brick.   I'd thought I did not know how to fight,
and all the years after I've believed I did nothing
but tremble there for him to steal, kill, eat my life.

Now, telling you this, I've remembered: Those nights
I slipped around, playing the detective, making my escape.

Then the boy and I at the kitchen table both began to grin.

At Fifteen, the Oldest Son Comes to Visit

1.

There it is: the indelible mark, sketched
on his belly, tattoo of manhood, swirled line
of hair, soft animal pelt, archaic design,
navel to hidden groin.   He squints, reaches
for a shirt, stretches in the tender morning
light high over me.   My shock is his belly
like my young body, abdomen swollen pregnant
and luxuriant with hair, a thick line of fur,
navel to cunt.   A secret message written on me
by him before his birth, faded, yet now surfaced
there with his body's heat, a physical thought,
a remark on my strict ideas about men and women.

2.

A judgment on the father who took the boy away,
to find me night, day, sitting there, the child
who looks like me, goes up the stairs on legs
skinny and long with familiar muscles, the boy
who brushes at my willful brown cowlick peak of hair.

Now he's stretched out immense on my bed, reading.
I see a cleft chin, angled cheek, his father.

Oblivious, he shifts, muscles bulk, knot, vanish
in his shoulders.   Since I left, he's shaped a self
stronger than his father.   His call one night:
Trying to make me think like him.   Last chance.
Soon I'll be too big.   I say I know that wrestle,
that invisible bending, the mind's mark on the body.

3.

I don't let him drive yet in the city, squalling
taxis, K Street, on our way to the misty river.

Red light:
                    Night, nine years ago, him yelling
in the back seat as we idle, braking at the light.
I rev the car, rattle of warped metal, and ask
why: *Why are you mad?*   We slip through the green.

Anger falls like a mask from his face, astounded
mouth.   Shaken into himself, he says he can't
remember, and laughs, I laugh, clangor of laughter
all the way down the boulevard, home.
                                              Dropped,
the guise of anger.   And whose face had he borrowed?

His father's?   Mine?   The mother who at his *No* had

grabbed with hands wider than his bony shoulders,
rattled him like a thin rickety door closed to me
I would open, I would.   This child who'd screamed
No, no the broken night I'd told I was leaving,

the almost-grown son beside me, smiling at the water,
the river, the slow sky mingling grey rivers of rain,

who doesn't remember much of then: his father's rant
and shove at me.   I'm afraid it is me he will hate
when finally some image opens like a mouth, anger
speaking in the long muscles of body like a tongue.

4.

This man by me who wears my body, younger, to
set out in, to set his mark on the world.

It's my anger that I'm afraid waits in him.
One day my face, as if mirrored, to grimace,

my head, my torso tower over, my hands
gesture, terror, like huge stones balanced

in bitter fury.   *But you don't seem angry,*
people say, not having seen me grapple a man

with words, my attempts to grip the throat:
my hands not yet able to take back my own,

reprisal, release.   I mean the broken body, raw,
the angry woman dead before her daughters,

her throat clasped with a red bright necklace,
purpling marks, a choker the two girls watched

their father fasten, a final feminine ornament,
with his own hands, to wring out her obedience

before she could leave the sharp edge of love.
And the girls?   They love their daddy, want to live

with him.   Why not?   They've seen who prevailed
when she did not and would not.   He's out of jail,

did twenty months, got judged fit as a father,
hadn't put a mark on them.   Why should they lie there

with the angry mother in the grave of clay?

Where she and I look up at the leaning-over faces:

Eyes far and sharp as malicious stars, a crowd
jeering, *Dirty, dirty, she's fit for nothing now;*

and silent ones who pile on stones; and the woman
who hands me a necklace, heavy, little stones,

babies' skulls, says, *Put it on;* the fluting air
of one: *Let the fathers raise them, in particular*

the boys; and the cold smart voice of a woman
saying, *It's simple, we have to stop loving men.*

From the bottom not so simple, looking back at when
I started out to leave him, when it was men against

women, looking up at the wet clay lumps mixed in
with bits of glass, mica, with insect chrysalides,

all flecks of light in the cold river of dirt
I am under.   The problem doesn't feel like love
but this weight that has buried me and the other.

To get out we gather the strength of the grave,
drink anger like water, eat sparks of grief:

the dead woman who rises up through granite,
the mother who splits the foundation slab,

the woman who brings down the tower, stones tumbled
like skulls. What skill can keep us unstruck?

Me, or the child who has choked under stones,
who has seen me walk among them, split and broken.

The fear is not love or anger, but a question:
What will he do with his hands?   At each gesture

I see his calloused palms and fingers, worn, cracked,
polished like river stone from months on the water.

I imagine him sculling his boat on the grave river:
the live water flinting, lingering in his wake

as he watches the fine crossings, the silver-
linked chains of oared water, form, dissolve behind him.

5.

He has my hands, wide palm, long fingers.
He has my big hands, which are my mother's.
Bit by bit our bodies gone on to our children,
like seed going to grass, long grass to seed.

Down by the river, the clumps of plume grass,
bearded grass in the setting sun, luminous,
delicate, hairy, taller than us this afternoon,
and my child taller than me by scant inches.

At a distance seen as man and woman, not son
and mother, walking, one of us at least wondering
how in the next years we might diverge from
those selves, those ideas.   The two of us talking
at the edge of a river flooded with warm rain,
yellow pollen foam, branches leafed-out green,
scraps of lumber splintered on the bridge: us

at this flux of violent water bound downstream.

Crime Against Nature

1.

The upraised arm, fist clenched, ready to hit,
fist clenched and cocked, ready to throw a brick,
a rock, a Coke bottle.   When you see this on TV,

robbers and cops, or people in some foreign alley,
is the rock in your hand?   Do you shift and dodge?
Do you watch the story twitch in five kinds of color

while you eat Doritos, drink beer; the day's paper
sprawled at your feet, supplies bought at the 7-11
where no one bothered you?   Or maybe he did.   All

depends on what you look like, on if you can smile,
crawl, keep your mouth shut.   Outside the store,
I, as usual, could not believe threat meant me, hated

by four men making up the story of their satiated
hot Saturday night and what they said at any woman
to emerge brash as a goddess from behind smoky glass,

how they won, if she would not bend her eyes or laugh,
by one thrusting question, broke her in half,
a bitch in heat, a devil with teeth for a cunt.

What's wrong with you, girl?   the grin, gibe, chant.
What's the matter?   (Split the concrete under her feet,
send her straight to hell, the prison pit fire,

blast her nasty self.)   *You some kind of dyke?*

Sweating, damned if I'd give them the last say,
hissing into the mouth of the nearest face, Yesss,

hand jumped to car door, metal slam of escape
as he raised his hand, green bomb of a bottle,
I flinched, arm over my face, split-second

wait for the crash and shards of glass.   His nod
instead, satisfied he'd frightened me back down
into whatever place I'd slid from.   Laughter

quaked the other men.   At me, a she-dog, queer
enough to talk?   At him, tricked by a stone-face
drag woman stealing his punch line, astonished

as if a rock'd come to life in his hand and slashed
him?   He dropped his hand, nodded like he'd won.
Slammed into my car, I drove away, mad, ashamed.

All night I seethed, helpless, the scene replayed,
slow-motion film, until I heard my Yes, and the dream
violence cracked with laughter.   I was shaken out

on the street where my voice reared up her snout,
unlikely as a blacksnake racing from a drain, fire-
spitting, whistling like a siren, one word, yes,

and the men, balanced between terror and surprise,
laugh as the voice rolls like a hoopsnake, tail
in her mouth, obscure spinning blur, quiet howl,

a mouth like a conjuring trick, a black hole
that swallows their story and turns it inside out.

For a split second we are all clenched, suspended:
upraised fist, approving hoots, my inverted ending.

2.

The ones who fear me think they know who I am.
A devil's in me, or my brain's decayed by sickness.
In their hands, the hard shimmer of my life is dimmed.
I become a character to fit into their fictions,
someone predictable, tragic, disgusting, or pitiful.
If I'm not to burn, or crouch in some sort of cell,
at the very least I should not be let near children.

With strangers, even one with upraised fisted hand,
I blame this on too much church, or TV sci-fi, me cast
as a mutant sexual rampage, Godzilla Satan, basilisk
eyes, scorching phosphorescent skin, a hiss of words
deadly if breathed in.
                        But what about my mother?   Or
the man I lived with, years?   How could they be so
certain I was bad and they were not?   They knew: the girl
baby fat and bloody from the womb, the woman swollen
stomached with two pregnancies.   My next body shift:
why did it shake them?   Breasts full for no use but
a rush of pleasure, skin tightened, loosened, nipples,
genitals gleaming red with unshed blood.
                                        I left
certainty for body, place of mystery.   They acted
as if I'd gone to stand naked in a dirty room, to spin
my skin completely off, turn and spin, come off skin,
until, under, loomed a thing, scaly sin, needle teeth
like poison knives, a monster in their lives who'd run
with the children in her mouth, like a snake steals
eggs.
        I've never gotten used to being their evil,
the woman, the man, who held me naked, little and big.

No explanation except: the one who tells the tale
gets to name the monster.   In my version, I walk
to where I want to live.   They are there winding
time around them like graveclothes, rotten shrouds.
The living dead, winding me into a graveyard future.

Exaggeration, of course.   In my anger I turn them
into a late-night horror show.   I've left out how
I had no job for pay, he worked for rent and groceries,
my mother gave me her old car.   But they abhorred me:

my inhuman shimmer, the crime of moving back and forth
between more than one self, more than one end to the story.

3.

The hatred baffles me: individual, doctrinal, codified.
The way she pulled the statute book down like a novel

off the shelf, flipped to the index, her lacquer-red
lips glib around the words: *crime against nature,* and yes,

he had some basis for threat.   I've looked it up to read
the law since.   Should I be glad he only took my children?

That year the punishment was: not less than five nor more
than sixty years.   For my methods, indecent and unnatural,

of gratifying a depraved and perverted sexual instinct.
For even the slightest touching of lips or tongue or lips

to a woman's genitals.   That means any delicate sip,
the tongue trail of saliva like an animal track quick

in the dew, a mysterious path toward the gates, little
and big (or *per anum* and *per os*), a pause at the riddle,

how tongue like a finger rolls grit into a jewel of flesh,
how finger is like tongue (another forbidden gesture),

and tongue like a snake (*bestial* is in the statute)
winding through salty walls, the labyrinth, curlicue,

the underground spring, rocks that sing, and the cave
with an oracle yelling at the bottom, certainly depraved.

All from the slightest touch of my lips which can
shift me and my lover as easily into a party on the lawn

sipping limeade, special recipe, sprawled silliness,
a little gnawing on the rind.   The law when I read it

didn't mention teeth.   I'm sure it will some day if
one of us gets caught with the other, nipping.

4.

No one says *crime against nature* when a man
shotguns one or two or three or four or five
or more of his children, and usually his wife,
and maybe her visiting sister.   But of the woman
who jumps twelve floors to her death, no I.D.
but a key around her neck, and in the apartment
her cold son in a back room, dead on a blanket:

Some are quick to say she was a fraud hiding
in a woman's body.   Some pretend to be judicious
and give her as an example of why unmarried sluts
are not fit to raise children.   But the truth is
we don't know what happened.   Maybe she could not
imagine another ending because she was dirt poor,
alone, had tried everything.   Or she was a queer
who hated herself by her family's name: *crooked.*

Maybe she killed the child because she looked
into the future and saw her past.   Or maybe
some man killed the boy and pushed her, splayed,
out the window, no one to grab, nothing to hide
but the key between her breasts, so we would find
the child and punish the killer.   The iron key
warm, then cooling against her skin, her memory,
the locked room.   She left a clue.   We don't know
her secret.   She's not here to tell the story.

5.

Last time we were together we went down to the river,
the boys and I, wading.   In the rocks they saw a yellow-
striped snake, with a silver fish crossways in its mouth,
just another one of the beautiful terrors of nature,
how one thing can turn into another without warning.

When I open my mouth, some people hear snakes slide
out, whispering, to poison my sons' lives.   Some fear
I'll turn them into queers, into women, a quick reverse
of uterine fate.   It took only that original slightest
touch of Y, of androgen, to alter them from girls.

Some fear I've crossed over into capable power
and I'm taking my children with me.   My body a snaky
rope, with its twirl, loop, spin, falling escape,
falling, altered, woman to man and back again, animal
to human: And what are the implications for the political
system of boy children who watched me like a magic
trick, like I had a key to the locked-room mystery?
(Will they lose all respect for national boundaries,
their father, science, or private property?)

In Joan's picture of that day, black, white, grey
gleaming, we three are clambered onto a fist of rock,
edge of the river.   You can't see the signs that say
Danger No Wading, or the water weeds, mud, ruck
of bleached shells from animal feasting, the slimy
trails of periwinkle snails.   We are sweaty, smiling
in the sun, clinging to keep our balance, glinting
like silver fishes caught in the mouth of the moment.

6.

I could have been mentally ill or committed
adultery, yet not been judged unfit.   Or criminal
but feminine: prostitution, passing bad checks.
Or criminally unnatural with women, and escaped,
but only if I'd repented and pretended
like Susan S., who became a convincing fiction:

Rented a two-bedroom, poolside apartment, nice,
on Country Club Road, sang in the choir at Trinity,
got the kids into Scouts, arranged her job to walk
them to school in the morning, meet them at 3:00 P.M.,
a respected, well-dressed, professional woman
with several advanced degrees and correct answers
for the psychiatrist who would declare her *normal*,
in the ordinary sense of the word.   No boyfriend
for cover, but her impersonation tricked the court.
In six months she got the children back: *custody.*
It's a prison term, isn't it?   Someone being guarded.

I did none of that.   In the end my children visit me
as I am.   But I didn't write this story until now when
they are too old for either law or father to seize
or prevent from hearing my words, or from watching
as I advance in the scandalous ancient way of women:
our assault on enemies, walking forward, skirts lifted,
to show the silent mouth, the terrible power, our secret.

Other titles from Firebrand Books include:

The Big Mama Stories by Shay Youngblood/$8.95

A Burst Of Light, Essays by Audre Lorde/$7.95

Diamonds Are A Dyke's Best Friend by Yvonne Zipter/$9.95

Dykes To Watch Out For, Cartoons by Alison Bechdel/$6.95

Eye Of A Hurricane, Stories by Ruthann Robson / $8.95

The Fires Of Bride, A Novel by Ellen Galford/$8.95

A Gathering Of Spirit, A Collection by North American Indian Women edited by Beth Brant *(Degonwadonti)*/$9.95

Getting Home Alive by Aurora Levins Morales and Rosario Morales/$8.95

Good Enough To Eat, A Novel by Lesléa Newman/$8.95

Humid Pitch, Narrative Poetry by Cheryl Clarke/$8.95

Jonestown & Other Madness, Poetry by Pat Parker/$7.95

The Land Of Look Behind, Prose and Poetry by Michelle Cliff/$6.95

A Letter To Harvey Milk, Short Stories by Lesléa Newman/$8.95

Letting In The Night, A Novel by Joan Lindau/$8.95

Living As A Lesbian, Poetry by Cheryl Clarke/$7.95

Making It, A Woman's Guide to Sex in the Age of AIDS by Cindy Patton and Janis Kelly/$3.95

Metamorphosis, Reflections On Recovery, by Judith McDaniel/$7.95

Mohawk Trail by Beth Brant *(Degonwadonti)*/$7.95

Moll Cutpurse, A Novel by Ellen Galford/$7.95

More Dykes To Watch Out For, Cartoons by Alison Bechdel/$7.95

The Monarchs Are Flying, A Novel by Marion Foster/$8.95

Movement In Black, Poetry by Pat Parker/$8.95

My Mama's Dead Squirrel, Lesbian Essays on Southern Culture by Mab Segrest /$8.95

The Other Sappho, A Novel by Ellen Frye/$8.95

Politics Of The Heart, A Lesbian Parenting Anthology edited by Sandra Pollack and Jeanne Vaughn/$11.95

Presenting. . .Sister NoBlues by Hattie Gossett/$8.95

A Restricted Country by Joan Nestle/$8.95

Sanctuary, A Journey by Judith McDaniel/$7.95

Sans Souci, And Other Stories by Dionne Brand/$8.95

Shoulders, A Novel by Georgia Cotrell/$8.95

(continued)

The Sun Is Not Merciful, Short Stories by Anna Lee Walters/$7.95

Tender Warriors, A Novel by Rachel Guido deVries/$7.95

This Is About Incest by Margaret Randall/$7.95

The Threshing Floor, Short Stories by Barbara Burford/$7.95

Trash, Stories by Dorothy Allison/$8.95

The Women Who Hate Me, Poetry by Dorothy Allison/$5.95

Words To The Wise, A Writer's Guide to Feminist and Lesbian Periodicals & Publishers by Andrea Fleck Clardy/$3.95

Yours In Struggle, Three Feminist Perspectives on Anti-Semitism and Racism by Elly Bulkin, Minnie Bruce Pratt, and Barbara Smith/$8.95

You can buy Firebrand titles at your bookstore, or order them directly from the publisher (141 The Commons, Ithaca, New York 14850, 607-272-0000).

Please include $1.75 shipping for the first book and $.50 for each additional book.

A free catalog is available on request.